CW00841519

A small little creature who struggles to see, is he flying up high, speeding fast past the trees?

Does he hang from his feet when having a nap?

Does he soar like an eagle when his wings start to flap?

A night flying animal who lives in the mud, not high in the sky reaching clouds high above.

Can you hear something moving and scratching around?

Who is this animal that lives underground?

Is it a hedgehog, a fox or even a cat?......

This is Alfie, a small friendly bat!
"A bat that lives underground?"
his neighbours all cry.
If only they knew this little bat is afraid to fly.

Alfie has put off flying for so long he is afraid if he
tries it, it might go all wrong.

"If I had courage, if I was strong, I would be gliding so gracefully and I would feel like I belong."

As Alfie stood wondering what it means to stand tall, he heard a strange tapping sound coming through the wall....

The sound he heard was travelling fast...

Alfie stood back and "yessssss!" cried a mole, "I have made it at last!".

"I have been on such a long journey you see, can I trouble you for some chocolate biscuits and tea?"

"Of course, hello there,
I'm Alfie and this is my hole".

"Good day, nice to meet you, I'm Perry the mole!".

"You smell a little strange, what are you, a rat?"

"Good heavens no, I'm Alfie the bat!"

"A bat?"

"Did you fall landing all this way down to the ground? I can imagine you have travelled and you have been all around".

" What does it feel like to fly in the air? To float like a feather with no worries or care?"

"Do you fly in the snow? Do you fly when it's raining? Does the wind on your wings feel truly amazing?"

"I would like to have stories, spread my wings in the sky, but to be honest with you Perry, I'm just too afraid to fly"

"My fear is if I try, I'll start falling and come crashing down to the ground like a brick."

"It's ok to feel scared and nervous but listen carefully, I might have a trick."

"Take a deep breath, hold my hand and I'll lead the way, follow me Alfie it's time to seize the day!"

"Come outside, close your eyes, take a breath, it feels right, believe in yourself, you're as light as a kite!"

"Your ears will guide you through the dark of the night, you will be flying at last and sleeping sound when it's light."

"Be brave and always be proud of who you are, you are Alfie the bat and a true shining star!"

"Now flap, flap your wings very fast, and feel your feet beginning to lift off of the grass!"

ALFIE

"Lift up your nose and point it high in the air, one more step
Alfie and you're nearly there!"

"Open your mouth and breath in with delight, that's it
Alfie you have started to take flight!"

"Look at me Perry! I'm going higher and higher! I feel as
mighty as a dragon that's breathing out fire!"

"What a special day this has been for me,
I'm so glad you popped by for biscuits and tea."

ALFIE

"Sharing my problem has made me feel free, I have also found a friend who believes in me."

"You look as small as an ant all that way down below. It's time for me to stretch my wings, I'll see you soon my friend but now I must go!"

"Fly away Alfie, fly as high as the moon, but remember come back, and visit me soon."